Above the Clouds

CHARACTERS

Narrator

Dan Daniels, news anchor

June Jasper, station manager

Henry Haynes, weather reporter

Amy Alvarez, scheduling clerk

Max Morrison, balloon mechanic

SETTING

The fictional town of Rainville, Washington, present day

Narrator: It is 12:22 in the afternoon in Rainville, Washington. We are inside the newsroom of TV station KBEC. The cameras are rolling as Dan Daniels, the news anchor, gives a report. Take it away, Dan.

Dan: And in local news, a man in a canoe was spotted paddling down Interstate 71 earlier today. It seems that the heavy rainstorm that took us all by surprise turned the highway into a waterway. Cars are backed up for miles. So if you have to be out in this storm, please drive—make that paddle— safely. We'll be right back with a weather update after this commercial break.

June: And we're off the air. I do hope Henry is prepared to give an accurate weather report.

Dan: Henry, your weather reports are all wet.

Henry: I don't make the weather, Dan. I only report it.

Dan: Incorrectly! That's the third day in a row you were wrong. You told everyone there would be sunshine!

Henry: Well, you know what they say. Three wrongs don't make a right—but three left turns do!

Dan: For a weatherperson, you're a clown.

Henry: Well, that makes sense, as I *am* also the host of the morning kiddie show here at KBEC.

June: As station manager, I would suggest that if you want to keep either job, your weather forecasts need improvement. When you say sunshine, there's a cloud cover. When you say calm, it is windy. People are getting seriously annoyed.

Narrator: Henry predicts, correctly for a change, that if he doesn't do a better job of forecasting, he'll be fired.

June: Stand by. We're on the air in three, two, one.

Dan: Welcome back to the KBEC noon report. Here's our weather clown—I mean, our weatherperson—Henry Haynes.

Henry: First, I'd like to apologize to Rainville. I know I predicted sunshine and blue skies for today. Instead, it has been pouring down sheets of rain. But as you can see on this weather map, it will be clear, gorgeous, and 85 degrees later this afternoon.

Dan: Excuse me, Henry. I think your map is upside down.

Henry: Oops! You're right. That's the weather for Mexico. Here in Rainville, we'll have tremendous gusts of wind this afternoon. The good news is, the winds are so strong that they will blow the clouds away. Tomorrow will be as dry as toast! Put away your umbrellas, Rainville, and take out your picnic baskets.

Narrator: The next day, because of Henry's forecast, the town park fills up with happy picnickers, including Henry and June. Around noon, the hailstorm hits. Unhappy picnickers run for cover.

June: Henry! This is unacceptable!

Henry: I know. Wrong again. Ouch! These hailstones hurt.

June: I believe I have a solution.

Henry: Run for cover?

June: No, I don't have a solution for the hail. It's a solution for your faulty forecasts. To report the weather correctly, you have to get on top of it.

Henry: You're right! I'll study my meteorology textbooks harder.

June: That's a good idea, too. But what I want to do is send you above the clouds so you can see the weather patterns forming. Then, you'll make better-informed predictions.

Narrator: June calls the Up, Up, and Away Balloon Company and rents a hot air balloon for Henry to ride. The next day, Max, the balloon mechanic, is doing a final check of the balloon outside the TV station. Amy Alvarez, Up, Up, and Away's scheduling clerk, comes by to tell Max and the news team that the pilot will be late.

Amy: Max, the balloon launch is delayed. The pilot has been sitting in a traffic jam on Interstate 5 for the last thirty minutes.

Max: Well, at least my part's completed; the balloon is ready to go up, up, and away! Are you going up this afternoon with the weather crew?

Amy: No, my job is to schedule the flights. Honestly, I'm afraid of heights. I prefer to stay here on the ground, far away from the balloon.

Max: So you've never actually been inside a hot air balloon? Climb inside the gondola and have a look around!

Amy: Well, I suppose it couldn't hurt. Only for a moment. I'm absolutely not going up in this crazy thing!

Narrator: Meanwhile, June and Henry prepare to broadcast live from the balloon. They arrive to load the balloon's basket with cables, cameras, microphones, and lights. While rushing around, June mistakes Max for the pilot.

June: Captain, it's time to take off. We're reporting live on the air in five minutes.

Max: Excuse me, but I'm afraid you're mistaken.

June: No buts! Let's blast off! Our ratings are going to skyrocket as high as this balloon.

Max: Whatever you say; you're the boss.

Amy: Wait just a second, I've got to get out!

Narrator: But there's no time to spare. Max pulls up the anchor and they lift off into the sky. Henry looks west through binoculars.

Henry: I'll watch the horizon for an oncoming storm.

Amy: As a representative of the balloon company, I must protest. You can't take this balloon into the sky without a licensed pilot at the controls!

June: Isn't he the pilot?

Max: That's what I was trying to tell you. Unfortunately, I'm just the balloon's mechanic. Fortunately, I am also studying for my pilot's license.

Narrator: So up, up, and away they go.

Max: It will be the coming down part that I'm not so confident about. We haven't reached that part in my class.

Amy: Oh, no! We're doomed!

June: Anyway, it's a little late to worry about that now. We're going live in three, two, and one! You're on, Henry. Have some fun!

Henry: This is KBEC's weather at noon, coming to you live from a hot air balloon. Off to the east, I can see a cloud accumulation. Clouds give us a lot of information about the weather. There are four main kinds of clouds: stratus, cirrus, nimbus, and cumulus. Those in the east are cumulus clouds, so I can tell that we will have a thunderstorm later today. If we can get to a higher altitude, I'll be able to show you even more clouds!

Narrator: Max hits the burner to heat up the air in the balloon. The balloon shoots up like a rocket.

Amy: Brrrr! It sure is freezing up here.

Henry: We're flying at eight thousand feet. At this height, we're above any rain clouds. We'll be back after this short break for more live weather from above the clouds.

Max: What did you say? My ears are popping.

Henry: That's because we're at such a high altitude. The air pressure pushing on the outside of our body is less than the air pressure on the inside pushing out. Air rushes out your ears to balance it.

Amy: My stomach is doing flip-flops. I don't feel so good.

June: Try to smile, anyway. You're on TV!

Amy: Ugh.

Henry: As the balloon climbs higher in the atmosphere, the air "thins." Your body isn't getting as much oxygen as it would at lower altitudes. So take deeper breaths.

Amy: *(breathing deeply)* In . . . out. In . . . out. In . . . out.

Henry: Feeling better?

Amy: I think so.

Henry: Good. Because as we go even higher . . .

Amy: I don't want to know! Oh, why didn't I become a dentist, like my mother wanted? Or a trombone player, like my father wanted? A nice job with both feet on the ground.

June: Okay, Henry, we're back on the air!

Henry: From up here, the weather and I can see eye to eye!

Narrator: Back at the KBEC station, the staff watches Henry and the hot air balloon on the screen. Dan Daniels is complaining.

Dan: This time Henry has gone too far! Reporting the weather from a balloon?

Narrator: Every phone in the TV station begins to ring.

Dan: There! I told you! The viewers are calling in to complain about that wacky weather reporter.

Narrator: But the viewers aren't calling to complain. They are calling to say how much they love Henry's report from the hot air balloon. They especially like that the balloon is now sailing out of control.

Max: The wind appears to have increased in speed and changed direction.

Henry: Hmm. According to my homemade weather vane, the wind is coming from the west and the south. That is usually good news, weather-wise.

Max: But it is not so good being-able-to-steer-wise. Hang on, I think we're in for some turbulence!

Narrator: The balloon dips. The balloon darts. The wind lifts the balloon higher and higher.

Max: The altimeter reads fourteen thousand feet.

Henry: I don't need an altimeter. We just passed the peak of Mt. Rainier. It's 14,411 feet high.

Amy: I'm so cold. Max, please, could you possibly turn up the heat?

Max: If you say so.

Narrator: Max turns the burner up as high as it can go. The balloon zooms up, up, up. It skims across the snow-topped mountain. Then it spins around and around and starts to drop.

Max: I hear a hissing noise. That's definitely not good news. I'm afraid the balloon has sprung a leak!

Narrator: The balloon drifts down, down, down.

Amy: This is a nightmare! We're falling!

Henry: But the barometer is rising. That's good news, Rainville. After this afternoon's rain, we will have dry weather tomorrow. It will be a lovely day!

June: Excellent forecast, Henry! You heard it here first on KBEC.

Amy: I hope we make it to tomorrow to find out!

Max: Don't worry, Amy, I have everything completely under control. I happen to have my trusty flight manual with me. Time for a quick study in landing!

Narrator: Max quickly flips to the last chapter of his hot air balloon pilot's manual. He safely brings the balloon in for a landing just outside the TV station.

Max: You can open your eyes now, Amy. And stop gripping my wrist so tightly! We touched down safely.

Amy: We made it? We made it! Hello, beautiful, solid ground. I will never leave you again.

Narrator: Dan Daniels and the KBEC crew run out to greet them.

Dan: Fine work, Henry. I owe you an apology.

June: What about the viewers? Did they phone the station? Did they complain?

Dan: They called, all right. And they loved the weather report! They want you to do it tomorrow the same way.

June: Excellent! Our ratings will go higher than . . .

Everyone: . . . a hot air balloon!

Max: Count me in! Absolutely! Once I get my real pilot's license, that is.

Amy: And absolutely count me out. I'll schedule the flights, but I refuse to go up again—not at that altitude!

Narrator: And from that day forward, right about noon, Henry Haynes's weather report was broadcast live from a hot air balloon.

Henry: Weather permitting!

 **The End**